NICK JR. The BACKYARDIGANS™
The Mighty Egg Sitters

adapted by Alison Inches
based on a screenplay by Adam Peltzman
illustrated by The Artifact Group

SIMON SPOTLIGHT/NICK JR.
New York   London   Toronto   Sydney

Based on the TV series *Nick Jr. The Backyardigans*™ as seen on Nick Jr.®

SIMON SPOTLIGHT
An imprint of Simon & Schuster Children's Publishing Division
1230 Avenue of the Americas, New York, New York 10020
© 2008 Viacom International Inc. All rights reserved. NICK JR., *Nick Jr. The Backyardigans*,
and all related titles, logos, and characters are trademarks of Viacom International Inc.
NELVANA™ Nelvana Limited. CORUS™ Corus Entertainment Inc.
All rights reserved, including the right of reproduction in whole or in part in any form.
SIMON SPOTLIGHT and colophon are registered trademarks of Simon & Schuster, Inc.
Manufactured in the United States of America
First Edition 10 9 8 7 6 5 4 3 2 1
ISBN-13: 978-1-4169-5039-4
ISBN-10: 1-4169-5039-7

In a faraway kingdom King Pablo struggled to pull off his crown.
"*Way* too tight," he said. He gave a great yank. "Whoops!"
The crown popped off of his head, and King Pablo tumbled across the
room just as his knights appeared in the doorway.

"Good timing, brave knights!" he declared. "I have an important challenge for you. You must guard this precious egg while I run out to buy a new crown."

The knights looked at the egg. Then they looked at each other.

"A challenge is battling trolls!" said Sir Tyrone.

"A challenge is saving a princess or facing a dragon!" said Uniqua the Knight.

"This," said Tyrone, pointing at the egg, "is not a challenge."

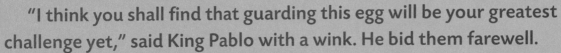

"I think you shall find that guarding this egg will be your greatest challenge yet," said King Pablo with a wink. He bid them farewell.

The trusty knights dutifully paced back and forth in front of the egg. As they did, the egg began to wobble. It wobbled off the pedestal and out the door. Then it rolled down the stairs.

"Catch that egg!" cried the knights.

The egg rolled out the castle door, bumped over the drawbridge, and bounced into the moat.

The fearless knights stared into the dark water. The egg bobbed to the surface and floated away.

"To the horses!" shouted Uniqua the Knight.

The mighty knights thundered along the river on horseback. They leaped over bushes and ducked under branches as they chased after the egg.

"Faster!" they cried.

But the egg slipped under some tangled roots and disappeared into the woods of the Grabbing Goblin.

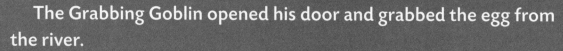

The Grabbing Goblin opened his door and grabbed the egg from
the river.

"Halt!" cried the knights. "We are the knights of King Pablo's court.
Hand over that royal egg!"

But the Grabbing Goblin took off with the egg.
"After him!" cried Sir Tyrone.

The knights chased the goblin through a long, dark tunnel and over a huge waterfall into a lake. The egg bounced onto the shore and cracked. Two legs popped out, and the egg got up and ran away—all by itself!

The egg ran straight into the forest of the Flighty Fairy.

"Hark, good fairy!" said Uniqua the Knight. "We are the knights of King Pablo's court—with a goblin in tow. We command you to give us that egg!"

The Flighty Fairy waved her magic wand and made the egg twirl and dance in front of her.

"Don't mess with the Flighty Fairy," she said with a laugh.

But the Grabbing Goblin *did* mess with the Flighty Fairy.
"Neato!" he cried as he grabbed her magic wand.

Suddenly, the egg began to fall!

"Abracadabra!" shouted the Grabbing Goblin as he pointed the magic wand at the egg. "Open sesame!"

But the egg fell to the ground.

Crack!
The shell cracked and sprouted wings.

"Look!" shouted Sir Tyrone. "The egg has wings!"
Then the egg flew away.

The two knights, the Grabbing Goblin, and the Flighty Fairy chased the flying egg. It flew to the top of Dragon Mountain—a place where no one dared to go. They came to a cave filled with bubbling hot lava . . . and there, perched on top of a boulder, was the egg.

Looming over all of them was an enormous dragon.
"Forward with haste!" shouted Uniqua the Knight.

The knights ran out onto a ledge and off the side of the mountain.

Aaaaaaaaaah!

A baby dragon swooped down and caught the falling knights on his back.

"The egg has turned into a baby dragon!" cried Uniqua the Knight.

The baby dragon flew everyone back to the castle.

King Pablo had just returned from buying his new crown.
"Did the egg give you any trouble?" he asked with a smile.

"Nah," said Sir Tyrone. "Well, maybe a little."
"All in a day's work," said Uniqua the Knight.

"Well done!" said King Pablo. "You have passed your greatest test. Only the bravest, toughest, and strongest knights can handle a dragon egg! But I have one more important question for you: What do you think of my new crown?"